Bad Habits!

Bad Habits!

(or,
The Taming
of
Lucretzia Crum)

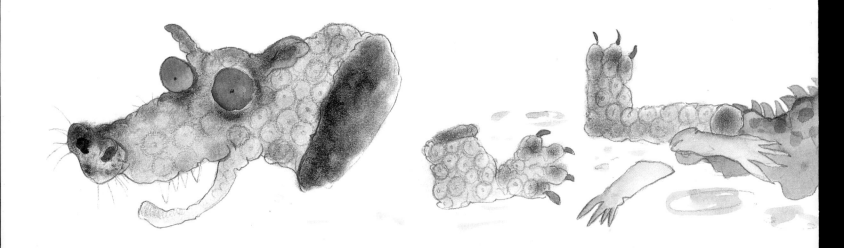

by
Babette Cole

Dial Books for Young Readers

New York

Lucretzia Crum was an uncivilized little monster!

She had disgustingly bad habits like . . .

BURPING

FARTING

and

SPITTING!

She yelled at her parents

and kicked and screamed if she could not get her own way.

She refused to eat at mealtimes, saying she'd rather starve than eat anything her parents cooked.

Then she'd sit in her room, munching on chocolates.

She stole from babies!

She pulled little girls'

pigtails!

The worst thing was that her school friends began to
copy her. They thought it was cool to be a
little monster like Lucretzia Crum!

"For goodness' sake, keep your daughter under control!"
the other parents said
to her mom and dad.

Luckily, Mr. Crum was a mad scientist.

So he set to work. . . .

He made his daughter the
"Blowfart Inhaler Suit."

The "Burp-bung."

The "No Scream/Kick Tube."

The "Thief-proof
Pullover."

And . . .

the "Pull-and-
wash Pigtail
Doll."

The
"Anti-foul-mouth Soap,"

"Spitting Cobra Ice Cream,"

and the "Classroom Pacifier"!

But as soon as her dad's inventions had been removed,
she became wilder than ever.

Even the cobra left home!

"It's my birthday soon and I want a party!"
demanded Lucretzia.
"Of course, dear," said her parents.
"We'll arrange *everything*!"

All the other little monsters turned up for the party and trashed the house.

Then there was a knock at the door and . . .

some really big monsters burst in! They wrecked the party. They spat, screamed, kicked, farted, and smelled far worse than the little monsters!

Lucretzia and her friends were scared.
"Who are they?" whined Lucretzia.

"Well," sighed her parents, "they were children once, but they turned into monsters because they grew up doing what you do!"

When the monsters had eaten all
the party food, they left, taking
Lucretzia's presents with them!

"We don't want to be a monster like you, Lucretzia Crum,"
said her friends, "if that's what happens to us!"

"Well, neither do I!"
wailed Lucretzia.

Mr. and Mrs. Crum were so pleased that they phoned the other parents to tell them the good news.

But they were having their own party, because their
monster trick had worked so well!

And Lucretzia Crum became

a civilized little angel!

First published in the United States 1999 by
Dial Books for Young Readers
A division of Penguin Putnam Inc.
345 Hudson Street
New York, New York 10014

Published in 1998
by Hamish Hamilton Ltd
Copyright © 1998 by Babette Cole
All rights reserved
Made and printed in Italy by de Agostini
First Edition
1 3 5 7 9 10 8 6 4 2

Library of Congress Cataloging in Publication Data available upon request